CHIMNEY
WITCH CHASE

CHIMNEY WITCH CHASE

Victoria Whitehead

Illustrated by Linda Fay North

ORCHARD BOOKS

A DIVISION OF FRANKLIN WATTS, INC.

New York

ORCHARD BOOKS

387 Park Avenue South
New York, New York 10016

ORCHARD BOOKS CANADA

20 Torbay Road
Markham, Ontario 23P 1G6

Orchard Books is a division of Franklin Watts, Inc.

MANUFACTURED IN THE UNITED STATES OF AMERICA

Book design by Tere LoPrete

10   9   8   7   6   5   4   3   2   1

The text of this book is set in 12 Monticello

Library of Congress Cataloging-in-Publication Data
Whitehead, Victoria.
    Chimney witch chase.

    Sequel to: The chimney witches.
    Summary: Ellen's efforts to get chosen for a school sports competition are complicated by the mischievous witch boy who lives in her chimney and likes to go for broomstick rides at the most awkward times.
    [1. Witches—Fiction.   2. Running—Fiction]
I. North, Linda, ill.   II. Title.
PZ7.W5858Cg   1988   [Fic]   88-1305
ISBN 0-531-05772-0
ISBN 0-531-08372-1 (lib. bdg.)

To the Witch Boy I knew once

Contents

CHIMNEY
WITCH CHASE

I

The Chimney

*E*llen was fed up.

"Richard forgot my birthday," she said indignantly as she and Mom watched Dad and Richard drive away. Richard was Ellen's older brother, and Dad was taking him back to Grandma's house where he would stay all week. He went to a special school to study music, and it was a long way away from home. Richard would be back again next weekend, but

Ellen's birthday was well before that, on Tuesday. Tuesday was also Midsummer's Day.

"I don't think he forgot your birthday," said Mom. "He's been saving up for a very long time and we've all chipped in so that he can buy you something special. Maybe you'll see Richard on Tuesday, that is if you get into the Midsummer Sports Meet."

The Midsummer Sports Meet!—of course, Richard would almost certainly be there. It was a big athletic meeting for schools, held in a town called Eardington. Ellen was hoping to be chosen to run for her school in the meet, but the tryouts were not until tomorrow. She would not be sure until after the tryouts whether she could go to the sports meet on her birthday or would have to stay at school. Suddenly, qualifying for the Midsummer Sports Meet began to seem like the most important thing in her life.

When Ellen went to bed that night, her little brother, Toby, came sneaking into her room and climbed into bed beside her.

"Go back to your own bed, Toby," said Ellen, yawning. "I have to sleep now, or I won't do well in the tryouts tomorrow."

But Toby did not want to go. She gave him a good push to get him started and he fell out of bed onto a rollerskate and hurt himself. He did not cry for long. He picked up a bicycle pump and waved it at Ellen, then he went across to the closed-up fireplace and pressed his ear against the bricks.

"I can hear noises," he said. "I think the Chimney Witches are going to do something soon."

"I certainly hope not," said Ellen.

Last Halloween she had discovered a witch called Weird Hannah living in her chimney—not only a witch, but a witch boy as well. His name was Rufus. The Chimney Witches did not bother Ellen much during the day but they were sometimes a nuisance at night. Tonight she hoped they would be quiet.

"No, Toby, nothing's going to happen tonight," said Ellen. "Go back to your room right now, or I'm telling Mom."

But Toby was still not ready to go to bed. He started playing around with Ellen's school bag and the pencil box inside it. She had left them on the floor near the fireplace, ready for next day.

"MOM!" called Ellen. "Come and get Toby, please. He's being a pest."

"TOBY! What are you doing?" said Mom, walking into the room suddenly and giving Toby such a shock that he accidentally spilled all Ellen's erasers out of her pencil box. The erasers rolled out of sight, under a bureau.

"Come on. Quick now," Mom went on as she straightened his hair and pulled on his pajama top. Toby hurriedly stuffed some marbles into Ellen's pencil box to replace the lost erasers, then he allowed himself to be led, grumbling, back to bed.

Ellen snuggled down under her quilt, just peeking out to take a last look across the room at the bricked-up fireplace. She listened carefully, but heard no noises—no shuffling or chuckling, no sneezing or shouting—none of the usual sounds that came at night from the Chimney Witches. She shut her eyes thankfully and was soon fast asleep.

2

The Party

*E*llen had not been asleep for long when she was awakened
by the sound of music and voices and bangings and
thumpings, coming from the chimney. She slowly opened her
eyes. There was a light shining across the room from the
landing, so she could see that the ornaments on her mantelpiece
were vibrating. There was a poster above the fireplace on the
wall against the chimney. It was a picture of puppies playing.
The noise was so loud that it was trembling too.

"The Chimney Witches," thought Ellen. Toby had been right. They were certainly up to something tonight.

She climbed out of bed and went across to the fireplace, banging on the bricks with her fist and calling, "HUSH! I'm trying to sleep."

There was no reply. Usually Ellen could hear Weird Hannah and Rufus arguing, but tonight the sounds were much louder and much harder to ignore. It sounded as if there was a party going on. Ellen wondered if it was someone's birthday.

"Rufus," called Ellen. "Whatever's happening behind there? What's going on?"

Still there was no reply. Ellen had an idea. There was an alarm clock by her bed with a very loud ring. She fiddled about with it for a minute or two, then she set it off. At the same time, she banged on the wall first with the rollerskate and then with the bicycle pump. The music stopped, then the witch boy's voice called through the wall,

"Hush yourself, Ellen, you're disturbing our party!"

"What do you mean—*I'm* disturbing your party!" cried Ellen. "It's *you* who's disturbing my sleep."

"Have it your own way," said Rufus, "but since you seem

to be awake, maybe you'd like to join us. Do you want to come over?"

Ellen did not feel like a party. It was too important for her to be in shape for tomorrow's sports tryouts.

"I'm not sure," she said hesitantly.

"Don't be a wet blanket," called Rufus. "Come on—all the goblins are here."

"The goblins," thought Ellen. "No wonder there's such a racket." Goblins love smashing and mending things. There is always chaos with goblins about. She wondered for a moment whether she ought to waken Toby and take him to the party too, because he loved the goblins and had a lot in common with them. Then she decided not to.

"All right," cried Ellen through the wall. "I'll come, but only for a minute or two."

Ellen had been visiting Rufus on and off since Halloween and she nearly always traveled from bedroom to chimney with the help of a spell rhyme and some spell powder. She knew that Rufus would be looking through his mother's things to find the right powder and she heard a rhyme like a faint echo inside her head:

"All the best
Of wishes hearty,
Ellen's coming
To our party!"

A dreamy feeling came over Ellen then. Her bedroom seemed to move slowly around her. The walls tilted oddly and, piece by piece, they fell away. There was a roaring, sucking, spining sound and a clatter like silverware being dropped into a stainless steel sink. Ellen felt herself turn over completely in a gentle somersault, then everything went dark.

Although she could not see, she somehow knew that her head was up a chimney and her feet were hanging down an open fireplace. She kicked her feet around to free herself.

She felt dozens of tiny hands grab her legs and the bottom of her nightgown, which had a green leaf pattern around the hem. The goblins tugged her down, and she fell heavily into the fireplace of a cozy parlor—the parlor of the witch in the chimney.

The parlor had tables and chairs and cupboards in it, and two beds, draped with bedspreads—a patchwork one and one which was sewn with stars. There was a witch's cauldron too. Usually it was bubbling with something hot inside, but not tonight because the witch in the chimney was not at home. Rufus, the witch boy, was there, grinning his usual broad grin, and twenty goblins were there too, giggling and hopping from foot to foot.

> *"Ellen's descended,*
> *Good witching, good Ellen.*
> *Gorblicious, Gorbleary,*
> *Here's cocoa, my dearie,"*

gabbled the goblins gaily. They all had fat bellies and spindly legs and never stood still for a moment.

The chief goblin, whose name was Bobgoblin, pushed a mug of steaming hot cocoa into her hand. Ellen, still not quite awake, raised the mug to her mouth.

"No, no!" squealed the goblins merrily. "Lorluvvagoblin, cocoa's not for drinking, it's for throwing."

You see, goblins love smashing and mending things.

"Oh yes, I forgot," said Ellen and she flung the mug wildly

across the parlor. It splattered cocoa everywhere and hit the witch's cauldron where it smashed to smithereens.

Rufus laughed.

"Tonight's the night for a party all right," he said, juggling with some bags of potato chips.

Rufus was a bony witch boy whose straw-colored hair stood up like bristles on a toothbrush. He wore black boots and gold and green striped socks. Especially for the party he was wearing a red and blue spotted bow tie that kept spinning around like a clown's.

"Who's the party for?" asked Ellen eagerly. "Whose birthday is it?"

"It's a Midsummer party for the Eve of Midsummer's Eve," Rufus told her.

"Oh, really? It's my birthday on Tuesday," said Ellen, just in case anyone wanted to know. No one did really, but they all sang "Happy Birthday, dear Ellen," twice, out of politeness, then the party began again.

Rufus put another tape on the tape recorder and jumped around to the music, drinking from a can of cola. The goblins shouted "yipppeee" and "here goes" and "yahooo" and began to throw things around. They threw things up in the air and down on the ground and into every carefully swept corner of the parlor. Jelly, cornflake clusters, and ketchup sailed gracefully through the air, twining prettily around candleholders and trickling stickily down walls.

Ellen sat down on a three-legged stool and nibbled at a bread roll. She was not really hungry and, although she did not want to be a wet blanket, she was thinking that she would almost certainly be better off in bed.

"By the way, Rufus," Ellen shouted over the blare of the music, "where *is* Weird Hannah tonight?"

Rufus's face clouded for a moment when he thought about his mother and the way her patience quickly ran out. He knew that she would not like what was going on in her usually neat and tidy parlor tonight. But Rufus never stayed gloomy for long and, after he had caught a flying flapjack and eaten it, his face brightened up again like a flashlight with new batteries.

"Actually, she's in Weirdeerie Wood with Uncle Whizoon," said Rufus. "He had an attack of gout and she's gone to look after him. She won't be back until after Midsummer's Night. Tonight's the night for a party all right. Am I right, goblins?"

"You're right," said the goblins and two of them slid by on a tuna fish sandwich, whistling "America the Beautiful."

Thinking about his mother being away, Rufus was struck by a brilliant idea. He made a dive for Weird Hannah's spare broomstick—the one she kept for emergencies, beside the vacuum cleaner and next to the mop and bucket.

"Who's for some roof races, goblins?" he cried. The idea went over well, and the goblins stopped throwing things and started dancing in a circle and jumping on and off the furniture.

> *"Roof races, roof races,*
> *Racket and riot,"*

they sang.

> *"Pop from the parlor,*
> *We're going to try it."*

Roof races sounded like a good idea to Ellen too. She thought that she might learn something to help her with the sports

tryouts the next day, so she got up from the stool and dropped
the remains of the bread roll into the cauldron.

When the goblins had circled first to the left and then to the
right and leapfrogged over each other, they formed an untidy
line and set off up the chimney as if they had springs under
their feet.

The Riot on the Roof

*W*hen they had gone, Rufus turned the music off, and he and Ellen looked at the mess the goblins had left behind. They thought briefly about clearing it up, but since Weird Hannah was not due back for at least two days they decided that there was no point. Rufus winked at Ellen and took a firm hold of her arm in one hand and his mother's broomstick in the other.

"Ready to go?" he said.

"Ready to go," said Ellen.

Rufus closed his eyes and looked important.

> *"What goes up*
> *Must come down,"*

he cried out loudly.

> *"But not until*
> *We've been to town!"*

"To town?" Ellen said.

"Well, roof doesn't quite rhyme, does it?" said Rufus, grinning. "But it'll be all the same, I expect."

There was a sound like a rocket blasting off and he and Ellen shot off up the chimney. They popped out of the chimney like toast out of a toaster.

Having found her footing, Ellen looked around and saw what a beautiful night it was up here on the roof. The moon seemed to be stuck on the dark blue sky like a stamp and the air was clear like new note paper.

"What do the witch people usually do on Midsummer's Night?" Ellen asked Rufus dreamily.

"A lot of them leave their chimneys in towns and gather in the country in Weirdeerie Wood," said Rufus, and there was a sound like wind rushing through trees. Ellen shivered a little and wished that she had brought her bathrobe with her. "But sometimes some of us have to stay at home," he added glumly. He looked down at the patched knees of his jeans and fiddled with the broomstick.

"Why couldn't you go to Weirdeerie Wood too?" asked Ellen sympathetically.

"Spell trouble," said Rufus. It was clear he did not want to say more. "Where are the goblins?" he said, changing the subject, glancing at Ellen, winking, and grinning all at the same time. "You can take part in the roof races too, if you like."

"I can't run here on the roof," said Ellen, "not dressed like this—in a nightgown and no shoes. Anyway it's much too slopey and slippery."

"Mmm," said Rufus thoughtfully, "I see what you mean. But you could with a spell. Yes. That's what I'll do. I'll teach you a speed spell. Give me a moment and I'm sure to think of one."

Now that was the best idea Ellen had heard all night. If she could learn a speed spell tonight, she could use it again in the morning, and then she would certainly be able to do well in the tryouts. She might even be able to beat Tabitha Arkwright. Tabitha Arkwright was the fastest runner in Ellen's school, and Ellen would be racing against her the next day in the 500 yard race. She told Rufus about that.

"No sweat," he replied. "I'll do you a speed spell to beat Tabitha Arkwright."

But it was silly of Ellen, really, to think things would be that easy. Tonight was the Eve of Midsummer's Eve and up here on the roof there were clusters of imps as well as gaggles of goblins.

Imps and goblins do not get on very well at the best of times, but tonight there was Midsummer Madness brewing, and the imps and goblins were overexcited. They started sticking their tongues out at each other and stepping on each other's toes on purpose. That led quickly to the hurling of insults and the throwing of anything else they could lay their hands on. As things got worse, pots and pans and cheese and pineapple and licorice and jawbreakers began howling through the air at great speed, ricocheting against chimneys and causing lumps on foreheads.

As Ellen and Rufus crossed the roof a piece of cheddar cheese got caught in the witch boy's hair.

"Yuck, I hate cheese," he said, pulling it out, dropping it on the tiles and treading on it.

"This is dangerous," said Ellen, ducking as a stick of celery whistled past her left ear. Rufus leaned his mother's broomstick up against a chimney and watched gleefully what was going on.

"Yes," he replied. "Good, isn't it?"

Ellen wondered what time it was and wondered if she shouldn't be getting home to bed.

"Rufus—about that speed spell . . ." she began.

But Rufus was not listening. He was looking around for some more action. He shouted "yahoooo!" and cartwheeled away. With the third cartwheel, he bumped into a cluster of imps who bundled him up and pushed him down the roof. He fell off the eaves but his shirt caught on a broken drainpipe and there he hung, swinging gently to and fro like washing on a line.

"I think maybe I should go home now!" Ellen called to Rufus from where she was standing, but he was much too busy aiming onion rings into a barrel of marigolds below to reply.

It was obvious to Ellen that she would get no more sense out of Rufus, no matter how hard she tried, so she thought that she would look for Bobgoblin. He might agree to do a spell to get her home instead. She weaved her way through the imp and goblin riot and eventually found Bobgoblin propped up against a chimney.

"Bobgoblin, would you please help me with a spell . . . ?" Ellen began, but Bobgoblin's head was reeling from a blow with a pan and he just turned and stared at her, cross-eyed.

"Over here!" yelled an imp called Jimmy. He was shouting at Bobgoblin, but Bobgoblin was too dazed to hear. It was Ellen who looked over at him. She did not see the jawbreaker flying toward her (even though it was a very big one with green and white stripes like a marble). But she felt it all right. She felt it when it hit her BANG in the mouth.

"OUCH!" she cried, horrified. The jawbreaker crashed to the roof tiles and Ellen spat out a jagged piece of tooth. Now she was furious too. "Just look what you've done!" she shouted at Jimmy the imp. "Just look what you've done to my tooth!"

When Ellen was angry, she had a very loud voice, and now she was very angry indeed. Her voice seemed louder than anything else that was going on. Everything stopped. The imps and goblins were struck dumb at the loudness of Ellen's voice. They dropped what they had in their hands or tossed it in the air or ate it.

"The goblins will mend the tooth!" cried the imps in a terrible panic, when at last they were able to speak again.

"No! I'd rather not!" said Ellen. She was afraid that the tooth might fall out altogether. "I'd rather go home!"

"Good idea," said Bobgoblin, who had been revived by the shock of her shout. "I think you'd better."

> "*Lorluvvagoblin,*
> *Children's teeth*
> *Drop like hail*
> *On folk beneath,*"

chanted the rest of the gang of goblins. Bobgoblin rubbed his head and jumped, turning like a ballet dancer in the air. When he landed again on the ground, he made a movement with his hands like two fish swimming down a drain, then he sang:

> *"Angry mob,*
> *Stop your gab.*
> *Off the roof*
> *With broken toof."*

"Broken 'toof'?" said Ellen, shuddering, but there was nothing she could do about the rhyme and she was prepared at that moment to put up with anything if only she could get back home to bed. Still with her hand over her mouth, she closed her eyes. She felt dreamy and drifty. Even as she slipped away from the roof she heard the sound of battle beginning again, but the noise drew away like daylight at the back of a railway tunnel.

When she opened her eyes again she was at home in the bathroom, sitting in the empty bathtub. She got out and looked at herself in the bathroom mirror. She saw that her tooth was broken and her lip looked red and sore. Not a good going-home present from a party on the Eve of Midsummer's Eve, she thought, and wondered why she had gone up on the roof in the first place.

"I'll never let Rufus persuade me to do anything, ever, ever again," she decided as she wandered back to her room and climbed sleepily into bed. She pulled her quilt up over her mouth and very soon she was sound asleep.

4

The Beetle

Next morning, when Ellen woke up, she felt with her tongue for her broken tooth. There seemed to be a jagged bit on one corner. She climbed out of bed and looked at her face in the mirror. There was a cut on her lip and the tooth was a funny shape. She did not want Mom or Dad to see it. They might think it looked like a job for the dentist.

Ellen did not like going to the dentist, but a trip there sometimes meant a day off from school. That was usually all right, but not this morning. Today was the day she had to run the girls' 500 yard race, and the winner would represent the school at Eardington. She had decided the winner was going to be her.

So at breakfast she held her hand across her mouth, just moving it slightly to squeeze her spoon in when it was full of Rice Krispies. She did not move her hand at all to speak.

"Sports tryouts today, Ellen?" asked Dad from behind his newspaper.

"Mmm," mumbled Ellen.

"Richard's running for his school, you know," said Mom, as she helped Toby take the top off his soft-boiled egg. Toby plunged his spoon into the shell and squirted egg yolk over Dad and the cat. The cat purred like a pneumatic drill.

"Mmm," muttered Ellen again.

"What's the name of that girl you've got to beat to get into the 500 yard race?" asked Dad.

"Mamama Marmite," said Ellen.

"Who?" said Mom.

"Mamama Marmite," said Ellen, louder but just as indistinctly.

"What's the matter with you, Ellen?" asked Dad. "Take your hand away from your mouth when you're speaking."

Ellen moved her hand away but kept her lips together like a ventriloquist.

"Mamama Marmite," she said even more loudly.

"Oh, you mean Tabitha Arkwright," said Mom.

"Yes," said Ellen, pleased, and she smiled broadly.

Toby squealed when he saw Ellen's broken tooth. Dad dropped the newspaper and Mom spilled her tea in the jam.

"Ellen!" cried Mom, "whatever have you done?"

Ellen could not tell her mom and dad that she had been caught in a brawl between some imps and some goblins, because they would think she'd been dreaming, so she said that she had fallen out of bed onto a rollerskate.

"It's nothing really," she insisted, wishing very hard that it had not happened. "I don't think I need to stay home from school."

But Dad thought differently.

"Look, Ellen, what time are the tryouts?" asked Mom.

"Mumma Memmon," mumbled Ellen.

"What?" said Dad.

"Half past eleven," Ellen shouted.

"We'll have you back at school by then," Mom said. "I'm going to ring the dentist now."

Ellen was given an emergency appointment for nine o'clock that morning.

"You look as though you've had an argument with a jaw-breaker," joked the dentist when he saw the broken tooth.

"A rollerskate," said Ellen guiltily.

The dentist smoothed off her tooth with his drill.

"Sorry I don't have time to rebuild the missing piece today," he said, but the tooth looked all right when he had finished. Ellen, Mom, and Toby hurried home so that Ellen could collect her things for school. Ellen dashed upstairs to find her school bag, shorts, T-shirt, and running shoes. When she opened the bedroom door she stopped because there, sprawled upon the bed, lay Rufus. His hands were behind his head and his feet, still in his boots, were against the wall. He was singing softly to himself, a song about imps and goblins, battles and bottles, teeth and trumpets.

"What are you doing here, Rufus?" Ellen said impatiently. "It's ten o'clock in the morning. You ought to be in bed."

"And you," said Rufus, "ought to be at school."

"I would be," said Ellen, "if you hadn't made me go up on the roof and get a jawbreaker in the mouth."

"Yes, I heard about that," said Rufus. "Why didn't you let the goblins mend it?"

"I went to the dentist instead," said Ellen. "It's safer." Mom called from downstairs. "Can't stop," said Ellen, stuffing her T-shirt and running shoes into a plastic bag. "We've got the sports tryouts in school today. I've got to get there as soon as I can."

Rufus sprang off the bed, just missing the rollerskate on the floor.

"Sports tryouts," he said, eyes bright like computer bleeps. "Is that like roof races? Hang on. I'm coming too."

"Oh, I wouldn't," said Ellen quickly. "The races aren't on a roof. They're not like witch races or goblin races. They won't be any fun."

She ran past Rufus and downstairs, but he overtook her, sliding down the banisters. He waited for her, grinning at the bottom. Ellen remembered that she was never going to let him persuade her to do anything ever again.

"Don't you want my speed spell to beat Tabitha Arkwright?" Rufus asked.

Ellen tried to push past him again. She didn't trust him. She didn't trust any boys much, but Rufus was worse than most. She considered for a moment, then shook her head and said, "Anyway, I can't take a complete stranger into school with me! It isn't allowed!"

"I'm not a complete stranger," said Rufus.

"To them you are," said Ellen.

"I can change myself into something not quite so strange if you like," suggested Rufus, "a beetle or something."

Ellen looked at Rufus's shining eyes and spiky hair. He was so cheerful and sure of himself that it was difficult to go on saying no.

"Well, all right," she said reluctantly, "but you've got to promise me that once we're in school there'll be absolutely no messing around. . . ."

While Mom was arguing with Toby in the kitchen over whether he should have another cookie or not, Rufus was preparing a beetle spell in the hall. He always carried magic spell powder about with him in case of emergencies. The powder he had with him today was all-purpose purple powder. It was in his back pocket and he thought it would do very nicely for a beetle spell.

But Rufus's memory was not good, especially when he was rushed, so he had a little trouble remembering the rhyme, even though it was one he had often done at Night Witchery classes. He bit his lip and wrinkled his nose because it helped him think, then he sprinkled some purple powder onto the stair carpet where it fizzled and moved about like ants. At last it settled in the shape of a star.

"Make Rufus small and smaller yet,"

began Rufus, thinking hard.

"He'll go to school as Ellen's pet
When I say . . ."

"Quick," Ellen broke in.
"Shh," said Rufus.
"But Mom's coming," said Ellen.

"When I say 'quick,' from big to little,"

Rufus continued,

"I'm going to shrink and be a bittle!"

"A bittle!" Ellen groaned.

"Well, beetle doesn't quite rhyme," said Rufus, "but it'll be all the same I guess." As he spoke there was a bang, a whistle, and a puff of purple smoke. Rufus's voice became higher and higher until it disappeared and he became a large black beetle running about the floor. Mom and Toby appeared, and Ellen scooped Rufus up and put him into her jacket pocket.

"I just hope you know how to change yourself back," she muttered.

"Pardon?" said Mom.

Ellen, Mom, and Toby went out through the front door. Toby stopped to poke a ladybug and watch it fly off a leaf.

"Come along, Toby," Mom said. "Be QUICK."

There was a loud pop and a puff of purple smoke and the sound of a ripping jacket pocket, and suddenly Rufus was walking down the garden path too. He tried to look casual and whispered to Ellen:

"This spell isn't working properly. I should never have tried to rhyme 'beetle' with 'little.' "

"I think it's the word 'quick,' " said Ellen.

Mom looked at Rufus oddly. He still had his bow tie on from the night before. She wondered how such a strange-looking boy had suddenly appeared. She looked inquiringly at Ellen, but Toby knew who Rufus was and he threw his arms around him, pleased.

"Oh, it's Rufus!" said Ellen, as if in surprise. "Hello, Rufus, would you like to come to school with us?"

"Thank you," said Rufus, and he set off down the garden path with a hop, a skip, and a jump. Toby tried to do the same. Mom followed and Ellen put her hand over her torn jacket pocket and hurried on behind.

5

The Spelling Test

*R*ufus and Ellen arrived at school at ten-thirty. They said goodbye to Mom and Toby at the gate and walked across the playground.

"I'm not taking you inside until you're a beetle again," Ellen told Rufus firmly.

"That's all right. I think I shall be in a minute," Rufus replied.

That was when he caught sight of the sports equipment in

the playground, ready to be taken to the field for the tryouts. In one bound, Rufus was beside the pile. Within seconds, he had thrown three javelins—one onto the roof of the school, one into the girls' locker rooms, and one into the sunroof of a passing car.

"Rufus!" cried Ellen, "you promised me, NO MESSING AROUND."

"So I did," said Rufus.

"We'd better be QUICK," said Ellen, and with a bang, a whistle, and a puff of purple smoke, Rufus became a beetle again. "Phew!" said Ellen thankfully. She took her pencil box out of her school bag and opened it. Then she picked up Rufus the beetle from the playground. She put him inside the pencil box and zipped him up. It was an old pencil box and there were plenty of holes through which he could breathe.

"You can stay in there for a while," she whispered through the holes, "and NO MESSING AROUND."

Ellen walked into class and apologized for being late.

"All right, Ellen," said Miss Pinn, her teacher. "You're just in time for a spelling test. Sit down and get out your pencil." Ellen sat down at her desk. A piece of paper was already on her desk in front of her. She opened her pencil box and Rufus waved an antenna at her as she took out her pencil. She quickly shut him up again.

"The first word I want you to spell this morning," said Miss Pinn, "is beetle. BEETLE." The whole class wrote down the word beetle. To Ellen's annoyance, she found that she had spelled the word BITTLE. She had to open her pencil box to look for an eraser.

She could see no eraser in her pencil box, only lots of marbles. She did not know that Toby had exchanged her erasers for marbles the evening before. As she hunted furiously among the pencils and marbles, the large black Rufus beetle came crawling out of the pencil box, across the top of the desk, down the leg to the floor, and out into the aisle between the other desks. The beetle waved first one antenna and then the other and looked around with interest.

Ellen eventually caught sight of the Rufus beetle. She bent down from her desk to try and stop him straying further. As she leaned over, the marbles rolled one by one out of her open pencil box. They rolled down the slope of the desk, sounding like fighter planes taking off, and then they clacked onto the floor with a sound like rifle fire.

The other children enjoyed this and began to kick the

marbles around the floor when they rolled near their feet. The marbles only stopped rolling when they reached the front of the classroom, and Miss Pinn's brown buckled shoes. Miss Pinn was too busy watching Ellen to notice. Ellen was still hunting for her eraser and trying to catch the beetle at the same time.

"Come along, Ellen. Settle down. Be QUICK!" said Miss Pinn. There was a pop and a puff of smoke and Rufus the witch boy was standing in the aisle in the middle of the classroom.

"I thought I told you not to mess around," hissed Ellen in alarm.

"I can't seem to help it," Rufus whispered back.

"Quiet!" said Miss Pinn, who was looking at her attendance book. A great hubbub arose in the classroom and Miss Pinn looked up and saw Rufus. "Who is this boy?" she said. "Is he a friend of yours, Ellen?"

"Yes, Miss Pinn," answered Ellen.

"What's your name, and why have you only just arrived?" Miss Pinn asked Rufus.

"Rufus, and I don't quite know," Rufus answered. Miss Pinn frowned over her glasses.

"Oh, all right then. Sit down next to Ellen," she said

irritably, "and you'd better come and see me at the end of the lesson." Miss Pinn found Rufus a piece of paper and a pencil, but Rufus was a strange-looking boy, who now had two antennae on his head and was still wearing a red and blue spotted bow tie. The class was finding it very difficult not to watch him and giggle. In fact, some of them got out of their seats to take a closer look.

"Settle down," called Miss Pinn. "Be quiet. Sit down." And most of the children returned reluctantly to their seats.

Tabitha Arkwright, who was taller than the other children, had longer legs and bigger feet than everyone else, and was wearing a very expensive track suit, did not return to her desk. She stayed next to Rufus, looking at him in a very superior way.

"He's got funny things on his head, teacher," she said, pointing to the antennae. Ellen fiddled with her socks and curled her hair around her finger.

Rufus did not take to Tabitha Arkwright. Very few people did. He steadily returned her stare with a witchy look in his eye, and spun his bow tie at her.

"Tabitha!" said Miss Pinn and, with a last suspicious look at Rufus, Tabitha sat down.

"And now," said Miss Pinn, "perhaps we can get on with our spelling test."

Rufus's eyes lit up. A spelling test, did she say? Rufus loved spelling. Spells were his favorite subject. Real school was not going to be so different from Night Witchery classes after all.

"Hey teacher, can I be the first one to do a spell?" he asked with great enthusiasm. Miss Pinn glowered.

"We shall all begin the test together," she said. "The second word I want you to spell is powder. POWDER."

"Yes. Yes. Here's my powder," cried Rufus, even more excited. And taking what was left of the purple powder out of his pocket, he jumped up out of his desk and ran to the front of the classroom. "Shall I levitate the table?" he asked.

"What a nerd!" scoffed Tabitha, but the rest of the class laughed delightedly. Miss Pinn sighed and pursed her lips, but when she looked at Rufus, his face was so full of cheerful expectation that she said, "Oh, all right, Rufus, spell levitate if you must, then sit down and stop making trouble!"

Ellen covered her face with her hair and sank down in her seat. The rest of the class chattered noisily and Rufus lifted his arm in a dramatic way.

He let a little of the purple powder slip through the fingers of one hand. It drifted to the floor and disintegrated in a shower of sparks. The class gasped.

> *"Lift your arms,*
> *Lift your eyes,"*

began Rufus mysteriously.

> *"Be still, and watch*
> *The table rise . . ."*

he went on, and stood with one arm in the air, head thrown back and gazing into the far corner of the room.

"What do you thing you're doing?" cried Miss Pinn in horror. "Rufus, this is a spelling test, not a conjuring show. Sit down immediately or go to the principal."

"I haven't finished yet," said Rufus. "There's more." He wrinkled his nose but, hard as he tried, he could not remember the rest of the rhyme. The class laughed uproariously and Ellen could not help smiling, but Rufus looked confused and hurt. After all, what was a spelling test for if it was not for testing spells? "I've got to say something like:

"*Rise and fall*
With gentle motion . . ."

Rufus tried again, but Miss Pinn then said "Rufus!!!" in a voice that sounded so like his mother's that Rufus felt quite sick and decided he would sit down after all.

But it was too late. The half-spell was cast. The table hiccuped a couple of times and slowly rose into the air. It hung in space, just in front of Miss Pinn's face. She marched furiously around the hovering table until she could be seen again.

"Put the table down immediately," she ordered.

Even worse was to come. Miss Pinn had interrupted Rufus's spell, and now she was involved in the muddle. The table thumped to the ground and Miss Pinn rose gently into the air. She hung about a yard from the ground, as if she was a puppet. Her face darkened. "Get me down from here," she commanded, like a queen, and down she came.

Unfortunately, when Miss Pinn came down, she came down on top of the marbles that had rolled out of Ellen's pencil box earlier. As her feet reached the ground they slid from under her. It was as if she was on rollerskates. Her feet went off in different directions. She did something like the splits, then sprang up and fell backward onto the table which was just sailing back up into the air.

Most of the class were saying things like "What a trick!" and "How did he do that?" but Tabitha was saying things like "This is really stupid," and "If we don't get on with the test we're going to be late for the tryouts."

"Rufus! Do something. QUICK!" Miss Pinn cried. But Rufus simply did not know what to do. This had not happened last time he had done the spell, so he was quite grateful when he felt the beetle spell coming on again. While everyone was watching the amazing floating table, with the acrobatic Miss Pinn on top, there was a muted whistle, a small bang, and a tiny puff of smoke and Rufus quietly became a beetle.

"Well, Rufus, if you refuse to put us down," said Miss Pinn, hanging over the side of the table like someone being seasick over the side of a boat, "you can go and explain to the principal. Rufus! Rufus? Where *is* Rufus?" Ellen was left sitting next to an empty space and gazing apologetically up at Miss Pinn who was swaying around somewhere between the window and the ceiling. The class was going wild with excitement.

"It's not like you to get involved in something as silly as this,

Ellen," called Miss Pinn as she drifted down to the windowsill. "Since Rufus has gone, *you* can go to the principal instead. *You* are the one who brought him here in the first place." With a sound like a dive-bombing airplane, the table bumped to the ground, then Miss Pinn climbed off it, straightened her glasses, and tried to look dignified. The spell was over. Ellen looked at the beetle on the seat beside her.

"You promised me . . ." she whispered through gritted teeth.

"What did you say?" asked Miss Pinn.

What *could* Ellen say that wouldn't sound silly?

"The principal's waiting for you, Ellen," grinned Tabitha. "Hurry now, or you'll miss the tryouts. No Midsummer Sports Meet for you." She looked around at the laughing children, who had never enjoyed a spelling test so much.

"Quiet, QUIET!" cried Miss Pinn. "Ellen, off you go!"

With a last indignant look at the beetle, Ellen left the classroom.

6

The Tryouts for the
Midsummer Sports Meet

The principal told Ellen that she would have to stay in at lunchtime and clean up the storage room as a punishment for fooling around in class.

"Well," Ellen thought, "at least I can make Rufus help me with that."

When she came out of the principal's office, the sports tryouts had already begun. She dashed straight to the locker room to put on her shorts and T-shirt and running shoes. But when she got there, she could not find the plastic bag with her sports clothes inside. She looked on and under every hook in the locker room, then she looked behind every radiator. Then she looked in the corridor and the bathrooms, but her sports things were nowhere to be found.

Ellen rushed out to the school field, to see how much time she had before the girls' 500 yard race, the one she wanted to win. She was dismayed to find that Mr. Box, the sports coach, already had the race organized.

"Come on, Ellen," he said, when he saw her. "I thought you wanted to represent the school in this event. You're not even changed."

"I had to see the principal," Ellen said, but there was no time for further explanation.

Tabitha Arkwright was all ready in her T-shirt and shorts and very large shoes, running on the spot nearby.

"Ellen's not fast enough to represent the school, Mr. Box," she said. "I'll run in the 500 yard race."

"Not if Ellen manages to do well in the tryouts, Tabitha," said Mr. Box firmly. "You're in almost everything else already." He looked at Ellen. "Five minutes, young lady," he said. "You've got five minutes to get changed and back out here, or I'm afraid you've lost your chance." Ellen ran helter-skelter back to the locker room, where she bumped into Rufus in the doorway.

"You promised me a speed spell," panted Ellen when she saw him. "A spell to beat Tabitha Arkwright. Will you do it now?"

"You're not even changed yet," said Rufus, and that was when Ellen noticed that, although *she* did not have any sports clothes, Rufus did. He was standing there in the doorway—bow tie, striped socks and boots were gone, and he was dressed up in T-shirt, shorts, and running shoes exactly the same color as Ellen's, and they did not seem to fit him very well either.

"Rufus, you're wearing my things!" said Ellen in disbelief.

"No I'm not," laughed Rufus. "I got these from the lost and found. No, *your* things are in Tabitha Arkwright's desk. I saw them myself and I saw her put them there!"

Rufus and Ellen raced back to the classroom and collected Ellen's things from Tabitha's desk.

"She's determined you're not going to beat her in that race," said Rufus.

"And I," said Ellen, "am determined I will. You prepare me the speed spell, and I'll go and get changed." Ellen did not need a speed spell to get changed in seconds. She was like greased lightning. She was soon standing beside Rufus, fully dressed in sports gear, and they had a minute left to get out to the field.

"Well?" said Ellen, "is the spell ready?"

Rufus had been searching frantically through his pockets and now he looked at her sheepishly.

"I'm afraid I don't seem to have any powder left," he admitted. "I won't be able to do the speed spell after all."

"Oh, Rufus!" said Ellen reproachfully. "I'm never going to beat Tabitha Arkwright now."

But Rufus screwed up his nose and began thinking hard. Perhaps he could take part in the sports tryouts too.

"Listen," he said, "I don't have any powder, but I've got a very good idea. I think I'm still partly beetle." Ellen looked at the two antennae stumps on his head and nodded.

"Well, if 'Qui . . .' I mean Q.U.I.C.K. is still the magic word, I think I know what we can do."

Out on the field Tabitha was doing knee bends at the starting point of the girls' 500 yard race. Ellen ran out, told Mr. Box she was ready, and took up her position. She had a big black beetle in her shorts pocket. She did not look down when she felt the beetle walk down her leg onto her shoe, even though it tickled. It was all part of the plan.

There were eight girls in the race. They lined up ready. Tabitha was next to Ellen and she smiled confidently at the other competitors. Ellen stretched her legs and rubbed her knees and smiled back up at Tabitha. Mr. Box raised the starting pistol.

"Are you ready . . . ?" he said.

"Yes, Mr. Box," said Tabitha, then she caught sight of the beetle on Ellen's shoe. . . .

"Mr. Box, there's a beet . . ." she began. But there was a loud BANG. Mr. Box had already started the race.

Ellen got a good start because Tabitha was so flustered by the beetle. But Tabitha had a long stride and soon caught up. She stuck out her elbow and pushed Ellen so that she almost lost her balance.

"That's for trying to scare me with a beetle," Tabitha hissed. Ellen cried out indignantly and stumbled but managed to keep going.

As they ran puffing and panting, side by side for a few yards, the beetle flew from Ellen's shoe and onto Tabitha's.

It ran up her sock and began to make a tickly feeling on her leg. Tabitha looked down at it and screamed. She flailed her legs and arms like a windmill and tried to kick it off, but it didn't help.

"Mr. Box, it's not fair, Mr. Box!" she cried, but she dared not stop running because Ellen was doing so well. She fell behind for a minute and that made her forget the beetle and run faster than ever. She caught up with Ellen again, ran past, and kicked her.

"Ouch!" Ellen shouted, and then she said sharply, "QUICK!" There was a whistle, a pop, and a puff of purple smoke, and Rufus momentarily returned to his real shape. He appeared on the track, merrily sprinting among the girls. He was right next to Tabitha. Rufus could run like the wind and had no trouble matching her pace. Tabitha turned her head and saw him and got such a shock that she once again lost her stride.

"Watch out for beetles, Tabby!" Rufus cried, and he winked and stuck his fingers up on his head and wiggled them about like antennae.

"Mr. Box, it's not fair," Tabitha wailed. While she was

distracted, Ellen raced ahead. She knew it was not fair, but neither was hiding someone's sports clothes in your desk. Summoning up even more energy, Ellen ran harder still.

Now the race was nearly over. Ellen looked around to check her position. She was at the front.

"QUICK!" she shouted again. Rufus popped and whistled and smoked and became a beetle. He scuttled off the track in case the runners trampled on him. Tabitha, not knowing whether to finish the race or chase the beetle, settled for the race. She approached Ellen for the third time and caught her. The race finished at the tape in a tie—a dead heat between Ellen and Tabitha Arkwright.

"Something very funny happened in that race," said Mr. Box, scratching his head thoughtfully as the girls gathered around him at the end of the race. They were all breathing heavily from their efforts.

"You can say that again," said Tabitha resentfully.

"We haven't got time to re-run the race," Mr. Box continued. "I think that both Tabitha and Ellen should represent the school in the girls' 500 yard race at Eardington."

Ellen jumped up and down in delight but Tabitha folded her arms and sniffed.

Mr. Box gave Ellen two large nines which the other girls helped her to pin on the front and back of her T-shirt. Tabitha was given two large eights.

"Well done, you two," said Mr. Box. "You both had excellent times. I expect you both to do credit to the school in tomorrow's Midsummer Sports Meet."

7

The Broomstick

*A*fter the tryouts were over, at lunchtime, Ellen had to stay in and clean the storage room. That was her punishment for what had happened in class that morning.

"You *are* going to help me tidy up the storage room, aren't you?" said Ellen to Rufus, who was just about to leave.

"Actually," said Rufus, "I'm a bit tired. I think perhaps I'll go back to my chimney and sleep," and he yawned with a noise that sounded like a sad elephant.

"But your mother's not there. I thought you didn't like to be alone," said Ellen.

"Oh, you're right," said Rufus, suddenly remembering how lonely the chimney could be when his mother was not in it. So while Ellen was cleaning up, Rufus roamed around in the storage room looking at this and that. After a while his eye was caught by a janitor's broom that stood in a corner next to a mop and bucket. The bristle part of the broom was almost a yard wide. He picked it up and stood astride the handle.

"You know," he said, "if I could find the right spell, I think I could make this broomstick fly really well."

"You don't have any spell powder," Ellen reminded him and, to make sure that Rufus did not get any further ideas about leaving, she picked up the plastic bag with her T-shirt, shorts, and shoes inside, and hung it over the bristles.

But once Rufus had an idea in his head it was hard to budge it. He put down the broom and sat crosslegged on the floor, flicking through the pages of a book called *Fun With Spelling*. Meanwhile Ellen, who was still busy cleaning, put some packages of glue powder onto a shelf. One of them dropped to the floor. Rufus threw the book aside and pounced on the package. He tore it open with his teeth, and poured half of it into his hand. He looked at Ellen and Ellen looked at him. His nose was beginning to wrinkle again, and Ellen started to worry.

Rufus now had a spelling book, some powder and a broom.

"It might just work," he said. "You know it might . . ."

"That's not spell powder," said Ellen anxiously. "It's glue powder for sticking."

"Then it may work for broomsticking," said Rufus. Keeping half the glue powder in the palm of his hand, he put the rest of the pack in his back pocket. Then he climbed astride the broom and, holding the glue powder and broomstick in one hand, he picked up the spelling book in the other. With a grand expression on his face, he said:

> "*A wood bough would bow,*
> *If sat upon now,*
> *While in storage*
> *In a storage room.*
>
> *A spell is a ticket,*
> *Glue powder'll stick it,*

A kick start'll trick it,
Now zoom away broom."

The book dropped with a thump and the glue powder slipped through his fingers. It sifted like sand to the floor. Ellen watched. Nothing happened immediately, but she knew that nothing often came before something big in Rufus's magical world.

There was a sound like shrink wrapping being pulled off, then the sound of a kick start on a motorcycle. The broomstick shook violently and the back went up. Ellen's bag swung around on the bristles, but it did not fall off.

"Yipppeeee!" cried Rufus. "It's going to work! Come with me, Ellen. Come to Weirdeerie Wood!"

"No," said Ellen, grasping a cabinet door firmly. "No, I'm not coming with you. I'm staying here."

The broomstick pulled back like you pull your arm back when you're about to throw a ball, then there was a roar like a jumbo jet as it rocketed out of the window and up over the surrounding trees. Ellen was left standing in a cloud of dust. There was nothing left of Rufus or the janitor's broom now except the smell of glue and bonfires.

Ellen could hardly wait for the last school bell to ring, so she could phone Richard with the good news about the race. But at last three-thirty arrived, and the bell jangled. She ran all the way home and she was just walking through the door when she heard the telephone. She rushed in and picked it up.

"Hello," she said breathlessly.

"Hi, El," said a voice at the other end. It was Richard. "Am I going to see you tomorrow at the sports meet, or not?"

"Yes," said Ellen proudly. "Actually, I'm going to be number nine. I tied for first in my race."

"How did you manage to do that?" asked Richard, laughing.

"Well, I did have a little help," Ellen confessed.

"Witch help, I suppose," said Richard.

"Sort of," said Ellen. "I lost my clothes, but I found them again, and in the end I won."

"Good," said Richard. "Then I'll see you at Eardington tomorrow. I've got a birthday surprise for you."

Ellen said goodbye and put the phone down. She was so excited that she jumped into the kitchen as if she was on a pogo stick. She could see from the look on Mom's face that she already knew what the surprise was to be, but she did not ask because she did not want to be told.

"I'm in the sports meet tomorrow!" she told Mom and Toby.

"Well done," said Mom.

"The bus leaves at nine-fifteen from school. I caught up with Tabitha Arkwright because of a beetle in my sock!"

"Excuse me?" said Mom, who was grating some cheese to put on top of the lasagna she was making for supper.

"Dad and I will bring Toby to the sports meet to watch you tomorrow," Mom told her, "since you and Richard will both be there. And Richard can come back with us for your birthday celebration."

"Oh good," Ellen exclaimed. "But I don't think I'll win my race. Tabitha Arkwright's much faster than I am."

"That doesn't matter," said Mom. "It's taking part in the race that counts."

Toby started jumping around as if he was on a pogo stick too.

"Toby, you look like a goblin," said Ellen. "Stop it. You're making me dizzy."

"There're goblins in my bedroom," said Toby, and there're goblins in the cupboard under the stairs."

"Well, you'd better get rid of them before tonight," said Ellen, "or we won't get any sleep, and I for one have got to make sure that I'm in good shape to do well in my race tomorrow."

8

Weird Hannah

But it was Ellen who did not get very much sleep that night. It was some time after midnight when she awoke with a start and sat up in bed so suddenly that her pillow fell to the floor.

She had been dreaming about running in the woods, and her nightgown was twisted around her knees. The thought suddenly came to her with a terrible jolt that she did not know where her shorts and T-shirt and running shoes were. She had lost her clothes for tomorrow's sports meet! She knew that she hadn't brought them home from school, but she also knew for certain that she hadn't left them behind. She picked up her pillow from the floor and hit the Mickey Mouse on it and wondered where on earth they could be.

That was when she heard the banging coming from the chimney. It was not unusual for her to hear noises. First she heard a bump and then a clatter and then an anxious mutter and then a shuffle and then another bump. Trying to ignore the noise, Ellen got out of bed to look for her sports clothes but, as she hunted among the things scattered on the floor, another thought struck her with another jolt.

Surely Rufus had gone to join Weird Hannah in Weirdeerie Wood. There should not have been anyone in the witch's chimney parlor to have been clattering and muttering and shuffling about.

But Ellen only wanted to do one thing now, and that was to find her sports things. She opened every drawer to look inside and had just got down on her hands and knees to look under the bed, when a scratchy voice from the bricked-up fireplace called: "Child from the real world, are you there?"

"Yes," said Ellen. She recognized the voice as Weird Hannah's. It seemed she must be there after all.

"Very well, I'm doing a spell to bring you over," said the witch. "Are you decent?"

"Yes," said Ellen. "I think so."

She looked down at her nightgown. It had a large acorn on the front and oak leaves around the bottom. It was a very decent nightgown. There was a bad-tempered cough from the fireplace and Ellen knew that a spell was about to be made. She closed her eyes and heard a rhyme echoing inside her head:

> *"Real children from the real world*
> *Make witches less than happy,*
> *But sometimes they just have to do,*
> *So come, and make it snappy!!"*

She stood by the chimney and waited for something to happen. There was a sound like things spilling out from a high cabinet. Something seemed to fall on her head, then she felt a swirling sensation. Within seconds she was under the table in the witch's parlor.

Weird Hannah was back from Weirdeerie Wood and was sitting on Rufus's bed, which was next to the cauldron. She was surrounded by the mess that had been left by the goblins the night before. She was chewing her fingernails and her hat was askew. It had been knocked crooked because she had been searching wildly through the chaos for something. Her witch's cloak was around her shoulders, and it seemed that she had just arrived or was just about to leave.

"Come on. Out of there," she said, when she saw Ellen underneath the table. Ellen crawled out and stood up. She smiled uncertainly, knowing that Weird Hannah had never liked her much. She did not like any children from the real world. Very few witches do. Weird Hannah closed one eye, stuck the tip of her tongue out of the corner of her mouth and put her hands on her hips.

"All right," she said, looking accusing, "what have you been up to this time?"

"Nothing," said Ellen, wide-eyed. She had no idea what the witch was talking about.

"Don't you play innocent with me," snapped the witch. "What have you done with Rufus?"

"Nothing," said Ellen again. "Rufus went off to Weirdeerie Wood. Actually, he was looking for you. He went on the janitor's broom. . . ." With a jolt, so strong that it made her head hurt, Ellen remembered at that moment where she had last seen her sports clothes—on the back of the janitor's broom!

"And . . ." she added in dismay, "he took my sports clothes with him."

"Weirdeerie Wood? He went to Weirdeerie Wood!" screamed Weird Hannah. "Oh disaster, oh calamity, oh catastrophe, oh no!" The witch threw her hat on the floor and jumped up and down on it until it became totally flat, then she threw her arms in the air, wailing loudly.

"I knew it! I knew it," she cried. "I knew that if I left him alone something unthinkable would happen!" She ran her fingers through her hair so that it stood out in all directions as if she had had an electric shock.

"Why? What *has* happened?" asked Ellen in alarm. She thought that she should try and comfort the witch but feared that she would only make things worse.

"Well—if you haven't got him," sobbed Weird Hannah,

"then he's a prisoner of the crabbiest witch in Weirdeerie Wood!"

"The crabbiest witch in Weirdeerie Wood?" said Ellen. She had not realized that witches came any crabbier than Weird Hannah.

"Yes," said the witch. "There goes Rufus's Midsummer down the drain, and mine and Uncle Whizoon's too, I shouldn't wonder. I just hope you're satisfied."

"I'm very sorry. I really am," said Ellen. She always found herself apologizing to Weird Hannah, even when she had done nothing wrong. What she was really thinking was that it was her Midsummer down the drain too!

"He always has had spell trouble with an old witch called Granny Crabapple," Weird Hannah went on, "and she said she'd turn him into a white mouse and put him in a cage if he ever went near her cottage again."

"Spell trouble," said Ellen. "I see." Everything was becoming clear now. Ever since she'd known Rufus he'd always had trouble with spells.

"Can I do something to help get Rufus back?" she ventured. "You see, when he went, he took something of mine."

"Of course you can't help," said the witch irritably. "You're from the real world, aren't you? People from the real world are no help to witches. Go home to bed. You're wasting my time. I've got things to do." And she picked up her hat from the floor and blew into it to make it the right shape again.

"But it was you who asked me to come here in the first place," Ellen protested. "And Rufus has got some things that I need for tomorrow!"

"Stop making a fuss," cried Weird Hannah, placing her hat back on her head and snapping the elastic under the chin. "If I can get Rufus out of that cage I won't let him out of my sight until after Midsummer."

And before Ellen could say anything else, the witch picked up her wand and poked her three times in the stomach. She made a noise like the air coming out of a balloon when you pull the mouthpiece narrow and muttered:

> *"Home to bed now,*
> *Stop the fuss,*
> *Today's the day,*
> *Don't miss the bus."*

Ellen did not even have a chance to say, "What bus?" With a feeling like traveling fast backward, she found herself back at home, sitting in the middle of the staircase, gazing through the banisters and wondering just what exactly she was going to do now.

9

Granny Crabapple

*E*llen was so used to strange goings-on that normally, if she had seen a goblin hop down the banister past her, she would have shrugged and ignored it, and normally, if she had seen a goblin jump through the cat door and into the kitchen she wouldn't have said anything at all. But tonight was different. When she heard some goblin-type jabber going on in her bedroom, she sprang upstairs like a kangaroo and ran into her room.

Bobgoblin was sitting on the end of her bed crossing and uncrossing his legs and looking embarrassed. Other goblins were sitting on shelves and hanging from lights and swinging gently on the curtains. They all looked uneasily at Ellen as she walked inside and snapped the door shut.

"All right," said Ellen. "What's happened now? What have you done with Rufus?"

"Nothing," said the goblins innocently, and they whistled and looked vaguely at the ceiling. Ellen waited, folding her arms and tapping her foot. "Well, the truth of the matter is," Bobgoblin said at last, "Granny Crabapple grabbed him."

> *"Crabapple jelly,*
> *Crabapple paste.*
> *A terrible moment,*
> *A terrible waste,"*

whispered the other goblins sadly.

"He's now a white mouse in Granny Crabapple's cage," Bobgoblin said, "and he will be until after Midsummer."

"She got in a rage
And he's stuck in a cage,"

added the other goblins, gathering around Ellen and Bob-goblin. So Weird Hannah had been right.

"But what did Rufus do to make Granny Crabapple so cross?" said Ellen.

"Just changed her witch's cottage into an apple pie," shrugged Bobgoblin as if it was something that happened every day.

" 'Twas just a little goblin brawl,
And Rufus made a spell
To change some house flies into pies,
The house got changed as well,"

sang the other goblins. They all began to do a sort of dance around the bedroom, but they were not their usual cheerful selves.

"We tried to rescue Rufus," Bobgoblin said, "but she made a goblin spell to keep us off."

"A spell, a spell.
A sneeze, a cough.
A spell can keep
A goblin off,"

the other goblins chanted.

"Well, *I'm* not a goblin," said Ellen. "Maybe I could rescue Rufus." The goblins stopped dancing, slapped each other on the back and fell about laughing.

"Lorluvvagoblin! You've got plenty of guts, but you're a bit short on wits!" exclaimed Bobgoblin. "In less than a trice, she'll turn you into a white mouse as well. You'll be lucky to be out of her cage by Christmas!"

"Gutsy witless
Run and hide,
Or stay inside
Till Christmas tide!"

giggled the goblins. Their spirits revived, and they sang their agreement loudly.

"But he's got my sports things, and he's locked in a cage,

and even if Weird Hannah gets him out she won't let him out of her sight until after Midsummer," said Ellen. "Somehow we've got to get him back from Weirdeerie Wood. There must be something we can do."

After a great deal of thought, everyone agreed that, dangerous as it might be, the goblins would have to go back to Weirdeerie Wood and take Ellen with them. All together, they might be able to confuse Granny Crabapple and snatch Rufus right from under her nose.

Goblin magic is not quite the same as witch magic. Ellen and the goblins all had to walk slowly around in a circle and say some gobbledygook together.

> *"Gobbling gabbling goblin*
> *Gnilbbog gnalbbog gnilbog*
> *Flee far fly*
> *Eelf raf ylf*
> *Flee far fly*
> *Be home by and by,"*

and it took a goblin's tongue to get around that one.

There was a roar and a howl like a high wind rushing

through poplars, and Ellen's bedroom spun around her like a tornado. When things stopped spinning, she found herself, together with the goblins, in a dark and tangled part of Weirdeerie Wood. The wind settled and the noise died. All Ellen could see was branches and blue-gray sky between them. All she could hear was the scuffling of squirrels, the hooting of owls, and the whisper of wind through trees.

The goblins led Ellen along a dark path that ran between brambles and nettles and came out at a clearing that was shadowy in the moonlight. There they left her. She stopped and stared for a moment into the clearing, because the sight that met her was very odd. It was just as if someone had plunked down a freshly cooked and very large apple pie in the middle of the wood. Its thatched roof looked as if it had sprinkled sugar on top. The pie was still steaming and Ellen caught immediately the delicious smell that wafted toward her.

It was so good that she could not stop herself from running toward the cottage. When she reached the door she broke off a piece of the knocker, and was about to eat it, when an ear-splitting voice like a faulty microphone screeched "DON'T" and all the creatures in the wood went quiet.

An old woman had appeared at the door of the pie. She was wearing a tall black hat and a spotted apron. She had two rollers in the front of her hair and a magnificent red, black, and blue wart right on the end of her nose.

"Don't eat Granny Crabapple's cottage, my duckling," she said, "or you could turn into a boiled carrot, or an old pie crust like me."

Ellen dropped her piece of pie like a hot potato and it shot stars in all directions and fizzled away on the ground.

"Tut, tut," said the old woman, shaking her head. "Don't they teach you anything at Night Witchery classes any more? Well—don't just stand there. If you've come to visit Granny Crabapple, you'd better come inside."

Ellen went in, and found herself in a witch's parlor, lit only by a candle or two and a crackling fire. All the chairs in the parlor were occupied by black witch cats, whose green eyes watched her moodily.

"Shooo," said Granny Crabapple, and the cats leapt into all corners of the room.

"Now, sit down, my turkey," said the old woman, "and tell me what brings such a pretty witch child to see a crabby old meatball like Granny Crabapple."

"Your white mouse," said Ellen boldly, "and some lost things of mine," and the firelight flickered on the old woman's face.

On the sideboard at the back of the parlor, there was a small glass cage with no door, only a glass lid in the top. The witch hobbled over to it, and Ellen went too. Inside the cage, she saw a white mouse with pink eyes and nose. He had a red and blue spotted ribbon around his neck, tied in a bow that kept on spinning around.

"That little mouse was a pretty witch child like you not so long ago," cackled the old woman. "What a shame." And she opened the lid at the top of the cage.

There was a large runny blue cheese on the sideboard next to the cage. Granny Crabapple squeezed off a piece and popped it through the hatch.

"Yuck," said Ellen when she smelled the cheese. "Rufus doesn't like cheese!" Then she slapped her hand over her mouth because she knew she shouldn't have said that.

Rufus as a beetle, a boy, or a mouse was as rude as always. With a kick like a star football player, he shot the smelly piece of cheese back out of the lid. It hit Granny Crabapple *splat!* on the wart at the end of her nose.

"Eeeek!" she screeched like an untuned radio, and Ellen covered her ears.

The witch looked down at the mouse with a look that would have turned jello to stale bread. Then, with a long breath that whistled in through her nostrils and out again through her ears, she snapped the lid shut. She looked at Ellen. She looked at the mouse again.

"You've come to rescue that mouse, haven't you?" she cried. "The pretty witch child has come to steal from the witch! I'll teach you to call on the crabbiest witch in Weirdeerie Wood, on Midsummer's Morn and well before dawn!" Ellen looked desperately around her and hoped that the goblins had not forgotten their part of the plan.

Just then there was a resounding crash as the goblins flung themselves against all the cottage windows, smashing the glass as they did so. They had clearly *not* forgotten.

"By the Great Wizard of Ages Ago," screeched the witch, "it's the Goblin Squad!" The goblins all danced around the old witch to distract her. Bobgoblin yippeeed with delight and yelled, "Ellen! Now!" as he sprang across the parlor to the mouse cage. When he reached it he gave it a tremendous karate chop, and smashed it to smithereens. Ellen dashed across to him and with two hands grabbed the white mouse who was sitting on a piece of broken glass and wiggling his nose vigorously.

"Where are my sports things, Rufus?" she whispered through the din.

"Everybody out!" cried Bobgoblin, and Ellen and the other goblins raced to the door and fled like rabbits from a shotgun.

Granny Crabapple's crabbiness reached a climax and the spell she made was a terrible one.

"Snarling dogs . . ."

she cried, whipping spell ingredients from the cupboards and tossing them into her cauldron which began to bubble furiously.

> *"Snarling dogs and wolves that howl,*
> *Scent of fox and stare of owl,*
> *Ere nightshade lights with poison dew,*
> *Children through their fear pursue. . . ."*

The cats turned into black dogs with muscular legs and flashing teeth. Growling and snapping, they threw themselves out through the cottage door and set off in pursuit of Ellen and the fleeing goblins.

10

The Chase

The goblins sprang like stags over thistles, and wove between bushes. Ellen found it difficult to run properly because she was carrying the white mouse cupped between her hands. She fell over the root of a tree.

"Wait for me!" she called. "I've fallen over." A hungry barking could be heard coming closer through the wood. The goblins were so afraid of the dogs that their fear made them deaf. They skipped on and away, higgledy piggledy, zigging and zagging, not knowing that Ellen had fallen behind.

She climbed awkwardly to her feet, still holding the mouse. Only a few yards further on, her foot caught on another root and she fell headlong into a thorny bush. The mouse ran from her hands and disappeared into a bush. Ellen lay still on the ground. The dogs could be heard very close now. She no longer knew which direction to go in. If she could not run from the dogs, she thought her best chance was to lie low, and hope they would run right past.

There was a terrific uproar as the hungry dogs hurtled by. She heard their feet scattering the dry leaves and barging through the underbrush but to her relief they did not stop. When the dogs had gone past, Ellen's heart was beating so hard that it felt as if it might jump out of her chest. After the noise, the wood seemed even quieter than before. She was not very comfortable where she was, but she was afraid to get up. She couldn't do anything but lie waiting for the goblins to come and find her.

But they did not come back. The dogs had gotten so close

to them at one point that they had all climbed up trees and sat in the branches with their heads together, trying to think of spells to change acorns into dog biscuits. They wanted to throw them down for the dogs. They hoped that this would make the dogs less hungry and less fierce so that no one would have to be afraid any more.

Ellen lay still in the bushes for a long time, thinking what she would like to do to the goblins if she ever saw them again. She was just beginning to realize that she would have to find her way home herself or miss her birthday, when she felt something small and warm brush against her cheek. She opened one eye and found herself looking straight into the two bright eyes of a mouse.

"Rufus," whispered Ellen, "thank goodness you've come back," and she struggled to her knees. Rufus wiggled his nose, raised himself up on his haunches, and moved his ears meaningfully from side to side. "Not that you're much help to me like that," she went on, stroking the mouse's head with her finger, "but at least you're company."

With something that looked like a wink, the mouse gave an extraordinarily loud squeak, whipped his tail around like the propeller of a helicopter, shot all four legs out stiffly in four directions, somersaulted three times, squealed like a firework and, with a BANG that sent Ellen reeling backward, disappeared completely. Standing in his place was a smug and smiling Rufus.

Ellen did not know whether to be relieved or annoyed.

"How did you do that?" she asked in amazement as she climbed to her feet and pulled thorns out of her hands.

"Easy," said Rufus.

"Then why didn't you do it before?" cried Ellen, exasperated.

"What, stuck in a spell-proof cage?" said Rufus. "If I'd grown big in that, I'd have crushed myself to death."

Rufus's explosion had drawn the attention of the dogs, and there was a hungry barking nearby. Rufus helped Ellen back to her feet, and together they set off through the wood, running like leaves in a storm.

"The janitor's broom," panted Rufus as they ran. "I left it in Uncle Whizoon's outhouse. His cottage isn't far. Stay with me and we'll keep ahead of the dogs."

But Ellen could not run as fast as Rufus. She had never wanted to be Tabitha Arkwright before, but now she felt it would not be such a bad idea.

"I need a speed spell," she puffed, as Rufus pulled her along behind him.

"No rhyme. No time. No chance!" cried Rufus, pulling her even harder. "This is training for your race today."

"Rufus, I can't," choked Ellen. She felt as if her lungs were going to burst. Rufus gave her hand a tug and guided her around some nettles and brambles.

"You could try saying things like SPEED, HASTE, DASH," suggested Rufus. "We *are* in an enchanted wood. It might just work. Don't give up. . . ."

"*Speed, haste, dash.*
Lightning flash,
Records smash,
Make a splash."

The dogs were getting closer.

As they approached Uncle Whizoon's outhouse, Rufus let go of Ellen and dashed ahead. The caretaker's broom was there and ready for flying. It still had the plastic bag with Ellen's clothes inside hanging on the bristles.

"Hurry!" cried Rufus. Ellen fell again, picked herself up and struggled forward.

"SPEED, HASTE, DASH," she said to herself over and over again, because she thought that if she did not, her legs would surely give way.

Rufus had the broom ready for flight by the time Ellen arrived. She jumped on behind him and hung on tightly. The dogs were within yards of them. Rufus still had half a package of glue powder in his back pocket. Without taking it out of the package, he threw it at the dogs. They gained precious moments while the dogs stopped to sniff it, hoping it was biscuits.

> *"Sight for sight,*
> *Sound for sound,"*

cried Rufus loudly, and the broomstick shuddered.

> *"Old witch folk say*
> *Up, up, away*
> *And off the ground!"*

Just as the first dogs reached them, the broomstick roared like a lion, pulled back like the strings of a bow and, shooting great clouds of smoke out behind, it took off and headed away through the trees.

The dogs snapped at the plastic bag on the back as it sped off. One dog caught his tooth in the plastic and pulled the bag so that a handle broke.

"What's in that bag?" Ellen asked.

"Your sports things," said Rufus.

"Thank goodness," gasped Ellen. "Thank goodness we didn't lose them!" As the broomstick sped clear of the trees, a twig caught the other handle of the plastic bag and it snapped. Down fell the bag. Down, down through the trees, disturbing bats and owls and sleeping squirrels as it did so. It landed back in the wood among Granny Crabapple's dogs, who sniffed it, hoping it was acorns.

Weird Hannah ran out of Uncle Whizoon's cottage.

"Rufus!" she cried. "Rufus, was that you and that real child too?"

But Rufus and Ellen were well out of earshot by then.

"Sit!" Weird Hannah shouted at the dogs, who were making

a terrible racket, growling and snarling at the sports things. The dogs took one look at the expression on Weird Hannah's face and sat down meekly in a circle.

"You're Granny Crabapple's cats, aren't you?" said Weird Hannah to the dogs. Now they were *really* confused. "By the Great Wizard of Ages Ago!" said Weird Hannah, shaking her head and patting the dogs until they purred. "What has that real child been up to this time?"

Rufus and Ellen arrived back at Ellen's house well before her mom and dad were awake. They flew in through her open bedroom window and landed comfortably on the bed. Ellen climbed off the broom and sat down thankfully on the Mickey Mouse pillow. It was good to think that it would soon be time to get up on her birthday and that, for now, all her troubles were over.

Rufus had jumped off the bed and was standing the janitor's broom up against the fireplace, bristle end up. He stretched and yawned like the call of a whale.

"Rufus, look!" Ellen said, and she suddenly got a feeling like the one you get when you jump off a swing and see that the pile of soft grass you thought you were jumping into has gone. Her relief vanished in a moment.

"Yes?" said Rufus.

"The plastic bag," said Ellen.

"Yes?" said Rufus.

"It's gone."

"Yes," said Rufus. "It fell off in Weirdeerie Wood. I think the dogs must have gotten it." Ellen could not believe what she was hearing.

"My sports things!" she shouted.

"Shh," said Rufus, "you'll wake your mom and dad."

"It's my birthday today," Ellen went on just as loudly. "I'm in the sports meet and you dropped my things in Weirdeerie Wood."

"I didn't drop them, they fell," said Rufus.

"Well, you'll have to go back and get them!" Ellen cried.

"I'm not going back to Weirdeerie Wood," Rufus said, with a shudder. "The dogs and Granny Crabapple are after me, and my mother's not too pleased with me either. I can't go back there. It isn't safe."

"I came to get you when you were a mouse," said Ellen.

"That's different," said Rufus.

"I cleared the storage room when you messed around in class," said Ellen.

"That's different too," said Rufus.

"I don't see why," cried Ellen.

"I'm *not* going back," cried Rufus, "and that's final!" Ellen climbed into her bed and pulled her quilt right up over her face.

"Then go away from me!" she shouted. "Go away! I don't ever want to see you ever, ever again."

Rufus thought at first that he would go away. But then he thought he would not. Ellen had never shouted at him like that before. Other people did—quite often as a matter of fact. Usually he didn't mind, but he did not want to add Ellen to the list of people who were angry with him. That was long enough already.

So, with a sigh, he picked up the broomstick. He also picked up Ellen's bicycle pump. He sighed again, this time very loudly. Then he said,

"Well, all right, if you're going to be like that, I'll try to get your things back. But it's going to be dangerous and I'm not going to promise." Ellen crossed her fingers tightly under her covers. She tried not to hope too hard or to trust him too much. "The school bus leaves at nine-fifteen," she said, quietly now. "I'll see you at school in the morning. Please, Rufus, don't be late."

Rufus decided that if he was going to be heroic, he might as well do it well. He waved the bicycle pump around like a knight waving a sword.

> *"No one is as smart as me—*
> *I'll get your running clothes, you'll see!"*

he shouted, climbing onto the windowsill.

> *"I'm Rufus and I never lose—*
> *I'll be back soon with Ellen's shoes!"*

he went on, getting astride the broomstick.

> *"In safety with this cycle pump*
> *In case into the dogs I bump!"*

He was enjoying himself now. He searched for some spell powder.

"With Whizoon's help, I tell no lie,
I'll change that crabby apple pie!"

He seemed to have finished for the moment. He found a few grains of purply, gluey powder, in a pocket he had missed earlier, threw them wildly about, and bent down and gave Ellen's quilt a good thump with the pump. The broomstick began to vibrate and smoke billowed out of the back. He made a spectacular exit through the bedroom window with a magnificent, star-shooting explosion.

Ellen shivered. All she could hear now was the sound of wind blowing through trees and Rufus's voice in the distance.

"I'll change that crabby apple pie
With Whizoon's help, I tell no lie.
So goodnight, Ellen and goodbye!"

The Midsummer Sports Meet

*N*ext morning, Ellen arrived at school at nine o'clock. The bus was waiting in the school parking lot to take the contestants to Eardington. Tabitha Arkwright was doing push-ups outside the girls' locker room. She was dressed in a brand new track suit with bright colored eights sewn all over it. She had a brand new sports bag packed with her numbered T-shirt, her shorts and her running shoes. Ellen was wearing jeans and sandals and was wondering whether her clothes were going to arrive in time for her to go. Some children piled into the bus. Ellen waited in a line with some of the others.

"Morning, Ellen," said Mr. Box.

"Morning," said Ellen.

"You've remembered your sports clothes, have you?" asked Mr. Box. Ellen mumbled something like yes, because she had *remembered*. It was not that she had *forgotten*. It was just that they had been dropped from a flying broomstick into an enchanted wood.

"Shall we have a clothing check, Mr. Box?" Tabitha Arkwright piped up, looking slyly at Ellen.

"Good idea," said Mr. Box. "Don't want anyone to arrive without anything." So, as everybody filed onto the bus, they showed Mr. Box their shorts, their T-shirts with their numbers on them, and their running shoes. Everybody except Ellen. She went to the back of the line where she stood looking anxiously around for Rufus. She looked around the playground, in the sky, behind the trees, and on the school roof. Where was he, she wondered. What could he be doing? She hoped he hadn't been put in a cage or eaten by dogs.

"O.K., young lady, where are your things?" said Mr. Box when he came to Ellen.

"They're coming," said Ellen.

"They may be coming," said Mr. Box, "but if they're not here now, they're already too late."

"I know," said Ellen, biting her lip.

"Well," he went on, "are you going to come without your things? If you do, you can't run. Or are you going to stay behind and wait—because we're leaving at nine-fifteen on the dot, clothes or no clothes, Ellen or no Ellen."

"I'll wait," murmured Ellen, and she looked down miserably at her sandals.

Ellen climbed onto the parking lot gatepost from where she had a good view of the sky and the road. Nine-fifteen came and went. Ellen could not bear to watch the bus pull out of the parking lot without her, so, when the engine started, she looked the other way. She heard the bus reverse and turn and drive unhurriedly through the parking lot gate. When she looked again, the bus was gone. The parking lot was empty. It was too late for her to go to Eardington. She jumped off the gatepost and kicked it so hard that a piece of brick fell off onto her toe.

"Who cares?" she thought. "Who cares if I've got a broken

toe as well as a broken tooth? I won't need to run today. In fact, I may not run ever again."

And that was when a cheerful voice behind her said, "Phew! I never thought I'd make it in time."

"You didn't," snapped Ellen, and without even looking at Rufus, she ran out of the parking lot, across the playground, and into the school. She had reached the door of her classroom when she heard the voice of Miss Pinn coming from inside.

"Settle down, class," she was saying. "This morning I'm going to give you an arithmetic test."

Ellen heard footsteps and turned to see Rufus hurrying down the corridor toward her.

"You're not coming into class with me," she said fiercely. "It's an arithmetic test and you'll hate it."

"No, I'm not going into class," said Rufus, "and neither are you."

"I've got to," said Ellen, "because I'm not running in the sports meet."

"But you *are* running in the sports meet," Rufus corrected her.

"Fat chance," said Ellen.

"You're not all that fat," said Rufus. "No reason why . . ."

"No reason?" Ellen broke in. "No shoes, no T-shirt, no shorts, no bus—how's that for a reason?"

"You really are a wet blanket sometimes," said Rufus. "What's wrong with the broomstick? Much more fun than the bus. I've got your stuff. I'll have you at the meet in time for the race."

"No," said Ellen. She was never going to say yes to Rufus, ever again.

"Oh, all right then," said Rufus with a shrug so big that his head practically disappeared into his shoulders. "I'll be going." And with a hop, a skip, a jump, and a somersault, he set off back down the corridor, leaving her standing alone.

Ellen knocked on the classroom door.

"Come in," called Miss Pinn, but Ellen did not go in.

"Come in," called Miss Pinn again. Still Ellen did not go inside. She started to smile instead. Then she looked at her sandals and laughed, quietly. Then she looked at the ceiling and laughed out loud. She turned away from the classroom and ran down the corridor as fast as her legs could carry her. She caught up with Rufus in the playground, and stood close to him, kicking a stone around with her toe. The toe was feeling much better now and clearly was not broken.

"Well, all right," she said. "I will come with you on the broomstick, but it's the very last time I let you persuade me . . ."

The janitor's broom sailed into the air like a dream. Ellen's clothes were in a fresh bag, and firmly secured on the back. The spell Rufus used was about old witch folk, sneezes, and guided missiles. The broom made a lot of noise taking off, but once up it was steady as an escalator, smooth as an elevator, and quiet as a hot air balloon. Rufus and Ellen flew higher and higher into the sky. When they were away from the town, they watched picnickers' hills and farmland slide below them. It was Midsummer's Day and the air was thick with a misty Midsummer excitement.

As they flew over forest, Ellen thought they must have reached Weirdeerie Wood. She leaned over to look down and try and pick out cottages. She saw a clearing and in it was a cottage that had a thatched roof which looked as though it had sugar sprinkled on it. There seemed to be dogs running around in the garden. There was definitely a cat on the chimney.

Ellen used one hand to hold her hair and stop it from flying around, and with the other she tugged on Rufus's shirt.

"Why did you take so long getting my things from Weirdeerie Wood?" Ellen asked. "Did you have a terrible fight with the dogs?"

"I'd rather not talk about it," said Rufus.

Ellen thought that he must have been very brave.

Rufus was steering the broomstick and so he was not able to tell her, just then, that the dogs had already become cats again by the time he got back, and finding the bag had been easy. It was slipping away from his mother that had been difficult. Weird Hannah had vowed not to let him out of her sight again until after Midsummer.

"Did Uncle Whizoon help you turn Granny Crabapple's pie back into a cottage?" Ellen asked. Rufus did a thumbs up sign and Ellen laughed with relief. "So I'm going to the Midsummer Sports Meet and you're going to be in Weirdeerie Wood for Midsummer's Night as well," she said.

"Yes," said Rufus. "Watch out!" He swooped down low over the nodding treetops. There was a cottage beneath which looked like Uncle Whizoon's. Weird Hannah was hanging up clothes in the garden. She looked up and seemed to wave, although she might have been shaking her fist.

Rufus yelled, "Back soon!" then he turned the broomstick to fly due north and in the direction of Eardington. When they were back in the open sky, Ellen tugged Rufus's shirt once again.

"About the speed spell . . ." she said. But Rufus saw a flock of birds ahead of them and he had to loop the loop to avoid them. After that there was a helicopter to fly around and then there was a kite with a long tail that looked like it might tangle them up. He had to concentrate all the time to keep them out of trouble. At last they were over the Eardington Sports Arena. It had a brown track and a green area in the center. Around the outside were stands fllled with spectators.

12

The Race

*E*llen was very excited when they touched down in the Sports Arena parking lot. She climbed off the broomstick and looked around at everything. Rufus yawned like a hungry hyena.

"Well, I'll be off then . . ." he said.

"What about the speed spell?" Ellen reminded him, but Rufus was already restarting the broomstick. He yawned loudly again. A cloud of black smoke belched out at the back of the stick and he was away. He flew off to Weirdeerie Wood for a long, long sleep at Uncle Whizoon's before he made merry on Midsummer's Night.

Ellen got changed and ran down to join the rest of the school team in the area at the center of the track. Mr. Box looked at her, puzzled. He wondered how she had gotten there. He felt certain that the bus had left without her. Tabitha scowled at Ellen, threw her track suit, all covered in eights, down on the ground, did a couple of push-ups and some ankle exercises and jogged to her starting position on the track. Ellen grinned at Mr. Box and followed. They had arrived just in time for the 500 yard race.

Ellen was once again next to Tabitha.

"No beetles down your socks?" sneered Tabitha.

"No," said Ellen.

"Then you don't stand a chance," said Tabitha. "I'm much faster than you."

Ellen knew that was true, but it did not matter. It was taking part that counted.

"Are you ready?" shouted the starter.

BANG went the starting pistol.

The girls set off. Tabitha made a brilliant start, but Ellen's was not good. She felt a sort of tiredness hanging on her like a coat with stones in the pockets. She thought it was because she had been awake in the night. Now everyone seemed faster than her. Not just Tabitha—everyone in the race. She willed her legs to move more strongly and her stride to be longer. She was at the back and struggling. A girl from another school who was wearing a number twelve on her shirt was running just ahead of her.

"Now what was it I learned in Weirdeerie Wood?" thought Ellen. "I managed to run there, when I thought I couldn't. SPEED, HASTE, DASH. Yes, that was it. SPEED, HASTE, DASH, LIGHTNING FLASH, RECORDS CRASH, MAKE A SPLASH!"

She muttered the words to herself once, then over again. She hoped they would give her the extra boost she needed to catch up with number twelve. Then at least she would not be last. They seemed to work. The way a bike speeds up when you suddenly reach the top of a downhill slope, she suddenly sped ahead. The weight left her. She passed number twelve, then number fourteen, then number seventy-three. She flew on like a leaf in a gale. She passed twenty-one, twenty-seven, thirteen, then two. Before she knew it she had caught up with number eight, Tabitha Arkwright.

Tabitha and Ellen were out in front, setting the pace. They were pulling away and leaving the whole field behind. Although Ellen had never gotten her speed spell from Rufus, and although she had been up for a lot of the night, she had been to an enchanted woods, and arrived at the sports meet on a magic broom. It seemed to her that she must have *some* magic left in her.

"SPEED, HASTE, DASH," muttered Ellen urgently. "SPEED, HASTE, DASH," over and over again, and she imagined there was a pack of hungry dogs behind her. With a fresh spurt of energy Ellen sprinted even faster. She was neck and neck with Tabitha Arkwright and within feet of the tape.

She glanced briefly up at the sky. It was a deep summer blue and full of moving dots. They might have been spots before her eyes or they might have been imps and goblins. There might even have been a broomstick up there too. Ellen was sure there was.

Her mind returned to the race. Three more strides and that

was it. She was through the tape. Her breath was coming so hard that it hurt. She threw her arms in the air, laughing triumphantly. She ran on a little, then bent over to get her breath back. She straightened and looked at the crowd, and only then did she begin to hear them. They were standing up and cheering at the tops of their voices. The finish of the race had been the most exciting of the day.

"Great stuff, Ellen," she heard someone cry.

"Well done!"

"Some finish!"

"Who won?"

"Tabitha."

"No, it was Ellen."

"I don't think it was."

"Who did win then?"

Tabitha was lying on her back on the ground with her legs in the air, shouting. She had never had to run so fast to stay in a race in all her life. Ellen knew she was the winner, but suddenly it didn't matter. It had been a fantastic race. She was here at the Midsummer Sports Meet, everyone was cheering, it was Midsummer's Day, it was her birthday and everything felt good! Mom and Dad and Toby were up in the stands and cheering too. They had come today to watch her run and they had seen her do a speed that was her lifetime best!

"I didn't know you could run as fast as that," said Dad when they were all together later in the spectator stands.

"I've been training," said Ellen, who was changed now and back in jeans and sandals.

"When?" said Mom. "In school?"

"No," said Ellen, "in the night."

"Excuse me?" said Mom.

Toby giggled and jumped up and down in his seat like a goblin.

Then Richard came running across the arena to join them.

"Well done, El," he said. "I didn't know you could run as fast as that."

Ellen smiled.

"Here's your present. We all chipped in to give you something special," said Richard, handing her a big parcel wrapped up in striped paper, with a brightly colored bow on the top—it was spotted red and blue.

"I'm sorry I didn't give it to you on Sunday. You must have thought I'd forgotten."

"No," said Ellen. "Of course not."

Ellen unwrapped the present eagerly. It was a brand new pair of running shoes, a pair of shorts, and a T-shirt with a number nine on the front and back. She was thrilled. She held the shirt up against her, put the shorts on her arm and the shoes on her feet.

"Like them?" said Richard.

"Oh, yes," said Ellen, "especially the nines."

"Now that you've got a spare set," said Richard, "if you lose one next time, you won't have to worry."

"That's right," said Ellen, and she danced about and clapped her hands and would have done a somersault if she'd been able to do one.

The family made their way together to the parking lot.

"Funny," said Richard, on the way, "I thought I just saw a boy on a broomstick fly over the arena and wave."

"Did you?" said Ellen.

"Don't be ridiculous," said Dad.

And everyone climbed into the car, ready for home.